Trolley *Dodgers* Pinstriped *Yankees* and Wearing

How MLB™ Teams Got Their Names

Jon Lindenblatt   Illustrated by Brian Kong

AMERICAN LEAGUE

Established 1903

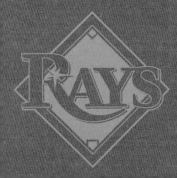

Baltimore

Orioles

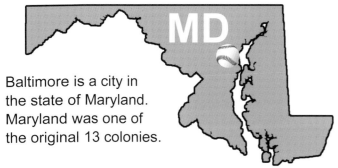

Baltimore is a city in the state of Maryland. Maryland was one of the original 13 colonies.

The team was named for the state bird of Maryland, the Baltimore oriole. The team colors are orange and black, which are the colors of an adult male oriole bird.

Cal Ripken Jr. played for the Orioles for 21 seasons. He is known as the Iron Man because he played a record 2,632 games in a row.

The Oriole Bird

The team began playing as the Milwaukee Brewers in 1901. The team then moved to St. Louis and was known as the Browns before moving to Baltimore in 1954.

The Sports Legends Museum at Camden Yards is located next door to the stadium and has exhibits profiling the history of sports in Maryland.

The Orioles play in Oriole Park at Camden Yards. The Park is located near the Inner Harbor, a historic part of downtown Baltimore.

BOSTON

MA

Boston is the capital city of Massachusetts and the largest city in New England. New England is the region of the northeastern United States that includes the states of Connecticut, Maine, Massachusetts, New Hampshire, Rhode Island, and Vermont.

In one of the most famous transactions in baseball history, the team sold Babe Ruth to the New York Yankees prior to the 1920 season. This led to the Curse of the Bambino. The Curse is the reason given by many Red Sox fans for not winning a championship for 86 years.

The team was originally founded in 1901 and was called the Americans. The Americans won the first World Series in 1903 over the Pittsburgh Pirates. The name Red Sox was later chosen by the team owner because of the red socks worn by the team beginning in 1908.

9

Ted Williams was the last player to have a batting average over .400 in a season. He is considered one of the greatest hitters of all time and won the **Triple Crown** twice during his career.

Wally the Green Monster

The Red Sox play at Fenway Park in Boston, Massachusetts. Fenway Park is the oldest stadium still used by any team in Major League Baseball.

CHICAGO

The White Sox play on the South Side of Chicago. The South Side is a major part of the city of Chicago.

One of the eight charter franchises in the American League, the team was originally called the White Stockings. The name was eventually shortened to White Sox. The team is also nicknamed South Siders.

Frank Thomas was a power-hitter who was known as the Big Hurt. He was a **designated hitter** who played on the team for 15 seasons. Only American League games are played with a designated hitter.

Southpaw is the mascot of the Chicago White Sox. A **southpaw** is a nickname for a pitcher who throws with his left hand.

In 1960, the White Sox were the first team to put their players' names on their uniforms.

The White Sox have played in U.S. Cellular Field since 1991. Before that, they played in the original Comiskey Park, which was named after the first owner of the team, Charles Comiskey. The first MLB All-Star Game was held there in 1933.

OH

CLEVELAND ™

Cleveland is a city in the northeastern part of the state of Ohio. It is located on the shore of Lake Erie, one of the Great Lakes. The Great Lakes are a group of five lakes located on the border between the United States and Canada.

The team has been called the Indians since 1915. Before that, they were known as the Bluebirds, Broncos, and Naps. The team had one of the first American Indian players in baseball, Louis Francis Sockalexis.

14

Larry Doby was the first African-American player in the American League. He twice led the league in **home runs.**

The Indians mascot is Slider. A **slider** is a type of pitch.

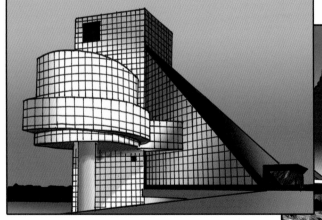

The Rock and Roll Hall of Fame is located in Cleveland. The first rock and roll concert was held in the city in 1952.

The Indians have been playing in Progressive Field since 1994. Before that, they played in Cleveland Stadium.

Detroit ™

Detroit is the largest city in Michigan and a major port city on the Detroit River. Lansing is the capital city of Michigan.

The team received permission to use the name from a military unit called the Detroit Light Guard, which was known as The Tigers. Before 1901, the team was known as the Wolverines.

Detroit is also known as the Motor City because the American car industry is based there. It is also known as Motown.

5

Hank Greenberg was a first baseman **slugger** for the Tigers who was inducted into the Hall of Fame. He was twice named the American League Most Valuable Player.

Paws

Ernie Harwell was the Tigers' broadcaster for 42 years.

The Tigers played in Tiger Stadium for over 85 years before moving to Comerica Park in 2000. There are two statues of tigers on top of the scoreboard in left field. Their eyes light up after a player hits a **home run** or the team has a victory.

HOUSTON

Houston is the largest city in Texas. Most American astronauts train in the city of Houston.

Astro means "star" in Greek. The team was named as a tribute to NASA, which is responsible for the space program, located in Houston.

Orbit

7

Craig Biggio was the first Astro to achieve 3,000 hits during his career. Getting 3,000 hits is an important milestone and is the mark of a great baseball career.

The Astrodome was the world's first domed stadium. Because the field was inside, **AstroTurf** was used instead of natural grass.

The team began playing as the Houston Colt .45s and changed its name when it moved into the Astrodome. The Astrodome was nicknamed the Eighth Wonder of the World.

The team has played in Minute Maid Park since 2000. The stadium has a retractable roof and a train theme. One of the main entrances is Union Station, Houston's former train station.

Kansas City

Royals

Kansas City is the largest city in the state of Missouri and is nicknamed the City of Fountains.

The Royals were named after the American Royal Livestock Show, which has been held in Kansas City every year since 1899.

5

Hall of Famer George Brett played his entire career with the Royals. He won the **Silver Slugger Award** three times during his career.

The team mascot is Sluggerrr, a crown-wearing lion. A **slugger** is a player who hits a lot of home runs.

The Royals began playing as an **expansion team** in 1969.

INTERSTATE 70

The Royals won their first **World Series** in 1985 when they defeated the St. Louis Cardinals. It was known as the I-70 Series because the two teams are both located in the same state and are connected by Interstate 70.

The team began playing in Royals Stadium in 1973. In 1993, the stadium was renamed Kauffman Stadium in honor of Ewing Kauffman, the man who founded the team.

ANGELS ™

The Angels were named after Los Angeles, the City of Angels, where the team began playing in 1961. "Los Angeles" is Spanish for "The Angels."

CA

The Angels play in Anaheim, a city in Orange County, California.

2002

The Angels won their first **World Series** title in 2002.

The Rally Monkey appears on the video board when the Angels are losing at home. It encourages fans to yell and cheer for the team.

The team is sometimes called by its nickname, the Halos. Halos are the rings that are sometimes shown above angels' heads.

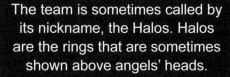

GO ANGELS

The Angels moved from Los Angeles in 1966 and now play in Angel Stadium of Anaheim. The stadium is referred to as The Big A and features a 230-foot sign with a halo. It lights up after every Angels victory.

MN

Minnesota™

The Twins play in Minneapolis, Minnesota, which is adjacent to St. Paul, the state capital. Minnesota is known as the Land of 10,000 Lakes.

In 1988, the Minnesota Twins became the first American League team to have 3,000,000 people attend their games during a single season.

The team was founded in Washington, D.C., in 1901 as the Washington Senators. When they moved to Minnesota in 1961, the team's name was changed in honor of Minneapolis and St. Paul, which are commonly known as the Twin Cities.

34

Kirby Puckett played center field for the Twins for his entire career. He won two **World Series** championships with the team and was inducted into the Hall of Fame. He was also named the Most Valuable Player of the 1991 American **League Championship Series.**

TC Bear

The Twins play in *Target Field*, which opened in 2010. Before that, the team played in Metropolitan Stadium and the Metrodome. The entrance to the stadium features statues of former Twins players, and downtown Minneapolis can be seen from the upper deck.

NEW YORK ™

The Yankees play in the borough of the Bronx in New York City. The Bronx is located across the Harlem River from northern Manhattan. The team is also known as the Bronx Bombers, which is a tribute to their power hitting.

The team began playing as the Highlanders in 1903 after moving to New York City from Baltimore. They were called the Highlanders because they played their games at Hilltop Park, one of the highest points in the borough of Manhattan. When the team began playing at the Polo Grounds in 1913, they became known as the Yankees. A yankee is a nickname for an American from the northeastern United States.

Derek Jeter has had more career base hits than any other Yankees player. He also has the most career base **hits** of any shortstop in baseball history.

The Yankees were the first team to have numbers on their uniforms. The famous pinstripe design of the Yankees uniform debuted in 1912.

There have been 14 **World Series** between New York City teams. These are called Subway Series because people can travel to games by using the subway system. The New York City subway transports people throughout the city and is one of the largest transportation networks in the world.

The team moved to Yankee Stadium in 1923 and started playing in the new Yankee Stadium in 2009. The original Yankee Stadium was nicknamed The House That Ruth Built. The name goes back to when Babe Ruth was on the team and hit many home runs.

CA

Oakland is on the eastern shore of San Francisco Bay in northern California. Sacramento is the capital of California. California has five Major League teams, which is the most of any state.

Oakland™

OAKLAND A's ATHLETICS ™

When the Athletics were formed in Philadelphia, the owner paid tribute to that city's first pro-ball team by using the same name as the first professional team in the city. The team is often called by its nickname, the A's. An elephant became the A's insignia in 1901 when an opposing manager told reporters, "The owner of this team has a white elephant on his hands." That phrase means that the opposing manager thought the team was expensive to own and not worth it.

34

Rollie Fingers was a **relief pitcher** that was known for his ability to **save** games.

The team mascot is named Stomper. He is an elephant who likes to enter the stadium on a little red car.

The A's play in *O.co Coliseum.*

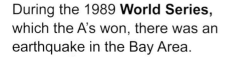

During the 1989 **World Series,** which the A's won, there was an earthquake in the Bay Area.

SEATTLE
TM

Seattle is in Washington state, located in the Pacific Northwest of the United States. The state is named after George Washington, the first president of the United States.

The Mariners are named for the maritime industry, which manages on the sea. Seattle is a major port city. A mariner is also an old-fashioned term for sailor. A sailor is a member of the crew of a ship or boat.

In 2001, Ichiro Suzuki became the first Japanese-born everyday **position player** in the Major Leagues. In 2001, he won the **Rookie of the Year** and **Most Valuable Player** awards.

Mariner Moose

The Nautical Compass Rose logo represents the sea, technology, and the great outdoors, all of which the Pacific Northwest is known for.

The Mariners are an **expansion team** that began playing in 1977. The team first played in the Kingdome, which was an indoor stadium. The Mariners have played in Safeco Field, which has a retractable roof, since 1999.

TAMPA BAY

The team was named for manta rays that are found in the water surrounding the Tampa Bay area. Manta rays are a type of fish and are sometimes called devil rays, the original name of the team.

The Rays play in St. Petersburg, Florida. St. Petersburg is part of the area known as Tampa Bay. A bay is a body of water that is partially surrounded by land but has a large opening with access to the ocean.

The manta ray is the largest of the rays and travels throughout the tropical seas of the world, typically around coral reefs.

Raymond

1998

The team began playing as an **expansion team** in 1998.

There have been more Major League **Spring Training** games played in St. Petersburg than in any other city.

The team plays home games at Tropicana Field, which is a domed stadium. The roof lights up with orange lights after every single Rays victory.

The Rangers are named after the law enforcement group who ranged or patrolled the Texas countryside and came to be known as rangers.

The Rangers play in Arlington, Texas. Texas became a part of the United States in 1845 as the 28th state.

The Texas Rangers mascot is Rangers Captain, who lives at Ameriquest Field in the tunnel right behind home plate. He wears number 72 on the back of his baseball jersey in honor of the team's first year in Texas.

Nolan Ryan, the all-time leader in **strikeouts**, finished his career with the Rangers in 1993. His nickname was the Ryan Express.

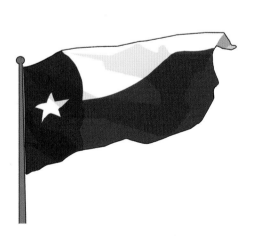

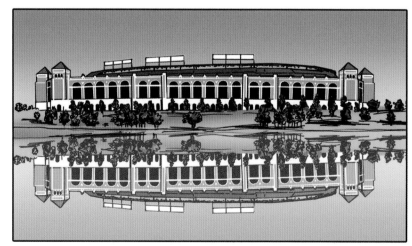

Texas is also known as the Lone Star State. There is a single star on the state flag because it used to be an independent republic.

The team originally played in Washington, D.C., as the Senators before moving to Texas in 1972. They began playing in Rangers Ballpark in Arlington in 1994.

TORONTO

The Blue Jays play in Toronto, Ontario. Ontario is a province of the country of Canada, which is located to the north of the United States.

The name of the team was chosen in a "Name the Team" contest. They are called the Jays for short. The blue jay is a species of bird native to North America and has blue feathering from the top of the head to midway down the back.

Joe Carter is known for hitting the **World Series** winning **home run** in 1993. He was only the second player to win a World Series with a home run in the bottom of the ninth inning of the final game.

The team's mascot is Ace. Ace is a nickname for a good starting pitcher.

The CN Tower is a well-known part of the Toronto skyline and was the world's tallest tower when it was built in 1976. The CN now stands for "Canadian National."

The team plays in the Rogers Centre, which was called the Skydome when it opened in 1989. The Skydome was the first stadium in MLB history with a retractable roof.

Established 1876

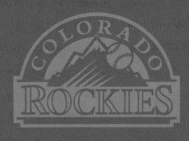

AZ

The Diamondbacks play in downtown Phoenix. Phoenix is the capital of the state of Arizona, which is located in the southwestern United States.

The team is sometimes called the D-Backs or the Snakes. The team colors are turquoise, copper, black, and purple.

20

Baxter the Bobcat

In 2001, the Diamondbacks won the World Series and gave Arizona its first major, professional sport championship.

Luis Gonzalez is one of the most popular players in Diamondbacks history. He had the game-winning hit in Game 7 of the 2001 **World Series.**

Diamondbacks are rattlesnakes that live in the desert. Most diamondbacks are poisonous with diamond-shaped markings.

The Diamondbacks first game was in 1998. *Chase Field* has a roof that can open and close.

Atlanta is the capital of the state of Georgia, which is located in the southern United States.

The team was called the Red Caps, Red Stockings, Beaneaters, Doves, and Rustlers before becoming the Braves in 1912. They were named after their owner, the Brave of Tammany Hall.

Greg Maddux won three **Cy Young Awards** in a row from 1993–1995.

From 1991 to 2005, the Braves won their division for 14 consecutive years. This is the longest streak in any professional North American sport.

Homer the Brave

The Braves are the only franchise in Major League Baseball to have won **World Series** titles in three different home cities.

The team played in Boston, Massachusetts, and Milwaukee, Wisconsin, before arriving in Atlanta, where they currently play at Turner Field.

CHICAGO ™

Chicago is the largest city in the state of Illinois and is known as the center of transportation and business in the Midwest. Chicago is located beside Lake Michigan, one of the Great Lakes.

The team has been known as the Cubs since the early 1900s. Cubs are the young of certain animals, including bears. They are sometimes called the Cubbies and the North Siders. The team was previously called the White Stockings, Colts, and Orphans.

Ernie Banks was the first player to have his **number retired** by the Cubs. He played his entire career with the team and was nicknamed Mr. Cub.

When the Cubs win a game, a flag with a blue "W" is raised on a flagpole in center field. When they lose, the flag has a white "L."

Wrigley Field was the last stadium to install lights. The first night game was played in 1988.

The team has played at Wrigley Field since 1916. The ballpark is famous for its outfield walls, which are made of brick and covered by ivy. Ivy is a green plant that grows on vines.

CINCINNATI

Cincinnati is located in the state of Ohio on the banks of the Ohio River.

The name of the team was chosen to remind fans of previous teams that played in Cincinnati. They were known as the Red Stockings and Red Legs before their name was shortened to Reds.

Johnny Bench won ten **Gold Gloves** in a row as a catcher while playing for the Reds.

Gapper

The Reds played the first night game in Major League history in 1935. That game was played at Crosley Field, the team's home from 1912–1970.

The first **professional** baseball team was formed in Cincinnati in 1869.

In 1934, the Reds became the first team in Major League history to use an airplane to travel from one city to another when they flew to Chicago for a game.

The Reds have been playing in Great American Ball Park since 2003. The park is located downtown and sits on the shore of the Ohio River. The stadium has a riverboat theme, which includes smokestacks in the outfield that launch fireworks when a Reds player hits a **home run.**

COLORADO™

They play in the city of Denver, which is the capital of the state of Colorado and is located just east of the Rocky Mountains.

1993

The Rockies began playing in Denver in 1993. Denver is nicknamed the Mile-High City because its official elevation is one mile above sea level.

The Rockies are named for the Rocky Mountains, which pass through Colorado. The mountain range stretches more than 3,000 miles between the countries of Canada and the United States.

Dinger, the team mascot, is a purple dinosaur. Dinosaur bones were found during the building of Coors Field.

The Rockies play in Coors Field. Coors Field is known as a **hitter's park** because the thin air allows balls to travel farther. Pitching is more difficult because balls don't **break** as much.

The 20th row of the upper deck of Coors Field is painted purple to show that it is exactly one mile above sea level.

In order to increase their weight, baseballs are placed in a humidor before Rockies games. A humidor adds moisture to the ball.

Los Angeles

Dodgers

The team was first called the Trolley Dodgers because of the train trolley cars that went through the borough of Brooklyn in New York City, where the team originally played. The name was then shortened to just Dodgers. They were also known as the Bridegrooms, Superbas, and Robins.

In 1958, the team moved across the country from New York to Los Angeles.

Los Angeles is the largest city in the state of California. It is known for being the home of Hollywood, the place where movies are made.

42

In 1947, Dodgers second baseman Jackie Robinson was the first African-American player in the Major Leagues. Jackie Robinson's uniform number has been retired by all Major League Baseball teams. He won the **Rookie of the Year Award**. The Dodgers have had more Rookie of the Year award winners than any other franchise in history.

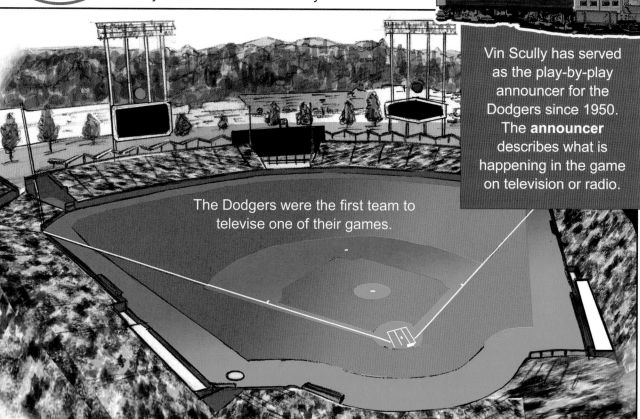

Vin Scully has served as the play-by-play announcer for the Dodgers since 1950. The **announcer** describes what is happening in the game on television or radio.

The Dodgers were the first team to televise one of their games.

The team plays in Dodger Stadium, which is located in the hills overlooking downtown Los Angeles.

MIAMI

Miami is a city in southeastern Florida located near the Atlantic Ocean. The Marlins began playing in 1993.

MIAMI

Marlins are large game fish. Marlins are found off the coast of Florida in the Atlantic Ocean.

1997

The Marlins won the **World Series** in 1997 after the shortest amount of time played by any **expansion team.**

The team mascot is Billy the Marlin, who got his name because the marlin is from the species known as billfish.

The Atlantic is the second largest ocean in the world. There are four major oceans in the world: the Arctic Ocean, Atlantic Ocean, Indian Ocean, and Pacific Ocean.

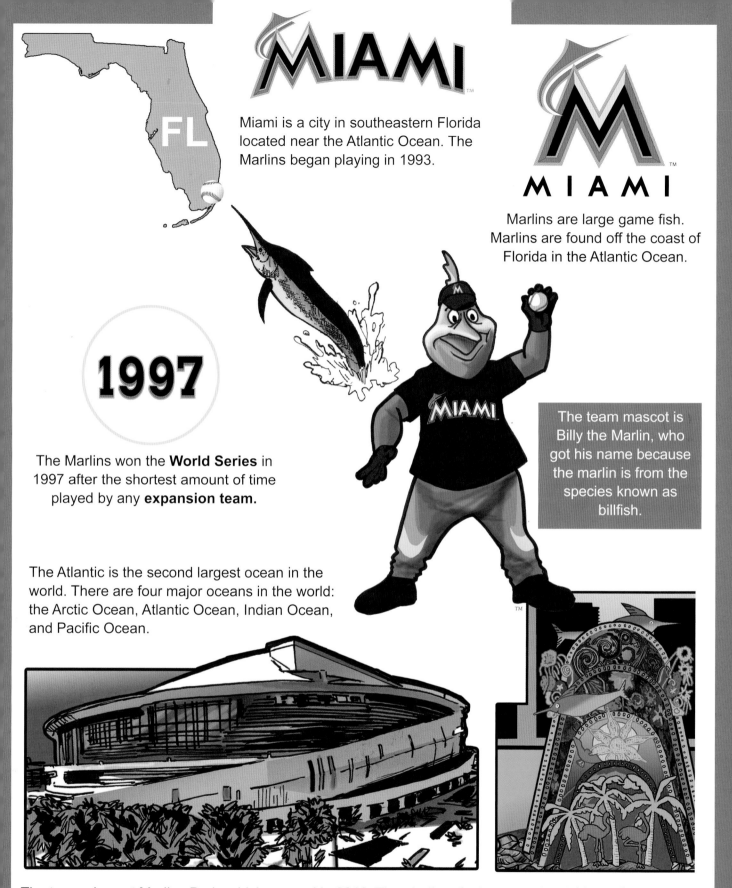

The team plays at Marlins Park, which opened in 2012. The stadium features a retractable roof, an aquarium behind home plate, and a display that goes off when a Marlins player hits a **home run.**

WI

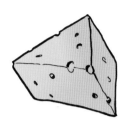

Milwaukee is the largest city in the state of Wisconsin. Wisconsin is known as America's Dairyland because it produces cheese and other dairy products.

A brewer is someone who makes beer. The city of Milwaukee was one of the top beer-producing cities in the world for many years. The team began playing in 1969 as the Pilots and moved to Milwaukee in 1970 after playing one season in Seattle.

19

Robin Yount is one of the best players in Brewers history. He won many awards and once **hit for the cycle.**

A race of sausage mascots is held at every home game and includes Brat, Polish Sausage, Italian Sausage, Hot Dog, and Chorizo who are called the Famous Racing Sausages.

The team mascot is Bernie Brewer. Each time a Brewers player hits a **home run**, he slides down a plastic yellow slide.

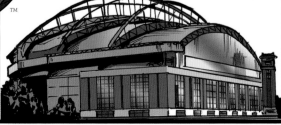

The team began playing at Miller Park in 2001. The stadium is one of the few stadiums with a retractable roof.

NEW YORK ™

The Mets play in the borough of Queens in New York City. There are five boroughs in New York City: Brooklyn, Queens, Bronx, Manhattan, and Staten Island. New York City is in New York state and is the largest city in the United States.

The name of the team is short for Metropolitan. A metropolitan is a person who lives and works in the city.

In 2012, Johan Santana pitched the first no-hitter in team history. A **no-hitter** is a game where one team does not get any hits.

The team colors are blue, orange, and white. The blue and orange are symbolic of the previous National League baseball teams in New York. The Brooklyn Dodgers wore blue, and the New York Giants wore orange.

Mr. Met, the team mascot, first appeared when the team moved to Shea Stadium in 1964.

The Mets began playing at *Citi Field* in 2009. Before that, they played next door at Shea Stadium.

New York is known as the Big Apple. When a Mets player hits a home run at *Citi Field*, a big red apple emerges from a giant top hat over the outfield fence.

Philadelphia

Philadelphia is the largest city in Pennsylvania. Philadelphia was the first capital city of the United States of America.

The team's name is a tribute to the city of Philadelphia and is the oldest team name in continuous use by any club in baseball. The Phillies were founded in 1883 and were originally called the Quakers. The original Quakers were a group of people who came to America in the 17th century to be free from religious persecution.

Mike Schmidt won three **Most Valuable Player (MVP)** Awards while playing for the Phillies.

Phillie Phanatic

The Declaration of Independence and U.S. Constitution were drafted and signed in Philadelphia. The Liberty Bell is also located in Philadelphia.

The team plays in Citizens Bank Park, which opened for the 2004 baseball season.

PITTSBURGH ™

Pittsburgh is in the state of Pennsylvania and is located near the Allegheny River. Pittsburgh is known as the Steel City because of their production of steel, which helped the city grow in size and importance.

PA

The team has been known as the Pirates since 1891 when the team was accused of stealing players from another team. A pirate is a person who plunders at sea. The team is also called the Bucs, which is short for buccaneers. Buccaneer is another name for a pirate.

21

Roberto Clemente played his entire career with the Pirates and had exactly 3,000 career hits. He was the first Latin American inducted into the Hall of Fame and was known for being a caring and giving person. Every year, the baseball player who best follows his example receives the Roberto Clemente Award.

The city of Pittsburgh's colors are black and gold. All the major sports teams in the city, including the Pirates, have black and gold on their uniforms. The colors are also found on the city's flag and seal.

Pirate Parrot

The team has played in PNC Park since 2001. The park is located along the shore of the Allegheny River.

SAN DIEGO ™

San Diego is located in Southern California and is the second largest city in the state. It sits just north of the U.S. border with Mexico.

The Padres are named in honor of the monks, or friars, who originally founded the city of San Diego. "Padre" is Spanish for "father" and is used to describe a priest. The team joined the National League in 1969 as one of four new **expansion teams** that year.

19

Tony Gwynn is known as Mr. Padre and won the National League **batting title** eight times.

The team is sometimes called the Friars because a friar is also a type of religious leader. The team mascot is the Swinging Friar.

San Diego is home to a world-famous zoo that is located in the Balboa Park section of the city. It is one of the largest zoos in the world with over 4,000 animals.

The Padres have played in Petco Park since 2004. The Western Metal Supply Co. building, which is a hundred years old, was made part of the stadium and serves as the left-field **foul pole.**

SAN FRANCISCO GIANTS

San Francisco is located on a peninsula. A peninsula is a piece of land that extends out into the ocean and is surrounded by water on three sides.

CA

The Giants were originally called the Gothams and joined the National League in 1883. After a big game the team's manager Jim Mutrie exclaimed, "My big fellows! My giants!" From then on, the team was known as the Giants. In 1958, after moving from New York, the team began playing in San Francisco.

24

Willie Mays played for the Giants in New York and San Francisco. He was known as the Say Hey Kid and was one of the best centerfielders in baseball history. Mays had eight seasons of at least one hundred **Runs Batted In (RBI).**

The city of San Francisco is also known for its trolleys and cable cars.

The Golden Gate Bridge was the largest suspension bridge in the world when it was completed in 1937.

The Giants began playing in AT&T Park in 2000. Before that, they played at Candlestick Park.

St. Louis Cardinals

MO

The team was founded in 1882 and was originally called the Brown Stockings. They have been called the Cardinals since 1900 when the team colors were changed from brown to red. The team is sometimes called the Cards or the Redbirds.

St. Louis is in the Midwest state of Missouri and is located near the Mississippi River. St. Louis is known as the Gateway to the West because many who moved west travelled through the area.

The Cardinals have won the most championships of any National League team.

Fredbird

6

Stan "The Man" Musial was known as one of the greatest hitters in baseball history. He was selected as an **All-Star** 24 times during his career.

A cardinal is a type of bird, usually found in the woods, that eats seeds and has a strong bill.

The Gateway Arch is a large structure located near the Mississippi that welcomes visitors to the city of St. Louis.

The team plays in Busch Stadium, which opened in 2006. This stadium is the third to be named after Gussie Busch, who bought the team in 1953.

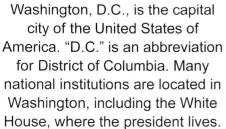

Washington ™

WASHINGTON NATIONALS ™

Washington, D.C., is the capital city of the United States of America. "D.C." is an abbreviation for District of Columbia. Many national institutions are located in Washington, including the White House, where the president lives.

The team moved to Washington in 2005 and was named after a team that used to play in the city.

Screech, the bald eagle, is the team mascot. The bald eagle is the national bird of the United States.

37

Stephen Strasburg was the first pick in the 2009 **draft.**

The team began playing in Montreal, Quebec, in the country of Canada as an **expansion team** in 1969. The team was originally called the Montreal Expos in honor of the 1967 World's Fair, which was called Expo 67. They were the first Major League team in Canada.

At every game at Nationals Park, the team holds a Presidents Race. The Presidents Race includes the four presidents of the United States found on Mount Rushmore: George Washington, Abraham Lincoln, Thomas Jefferson, and Theodore Roosevelt.

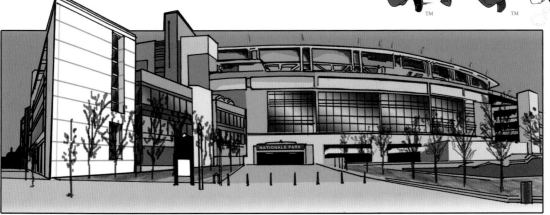

The team plays in Nationals Park, which is located along the Anacostia River. The Washington Monument and Capitol Building can be seen from inside the stadium.

For my wife and best friend, Shira, who patiently deals with the other love in my life, baseball. For my sons, Ben Jagger and Ryan Bruce, who are going to be very upset when they find out they're Mets fans.

-Jon Lindenblatt

Dedicated to Cindy. Thanks for always being there. And to our Summer Jade. Love you both! For baseball fans everywhere, enjoy!

-Brian Kong

Have a book idea?

Contact us at: Mascot Books

560 Herndon Parkway Suite 120, Herndon, VA 20170

info@mascotbooks.com | www.mascotbooks.com

Trolley Dodgers, Pinstriped Yankees, and Wearing Red Sox

Major League Baseball trademarks and copyrights are used with permission of Major League Baseball Properties, Inc. Visit MLB.com

Book © 2013 by Jon Lindenblatt

PRT0313A

Printed in the United States

ISBN-13: 9781620860595
ISBN-10: 1620860597

www.mascotbooks.com